and Little Crumb's
Really Big Footy Game

Look out for more Frankly Frank books:

Frankly Frank and the
Unidentified Flying Blob

Frankly Frank

and Little Crumb's
Really Big Footy Game

DAMON BURNARD

■SCHOLASTIC

Scholastic Children's Books,
Commonwealth House, 1-19 New Oxford Street,
London, WC1A 1NU, UK
a division of Scholastic Ltd
London ~ New York ~ Toronto ~ Sydney ~ Auckland
Mexico City ~ New Delhi ~ Hong Kong

First published by Scholastic Ltd, 2004

ISBN 0 439 97344 9

Printed and bound by AIT Nørhaven A/S, Denmark

2 4 6 8 10 9 7 5 3 1

CHAPTER ONE

Once upon a Saturday, Frank and his friends were playing football.

Their team's name was Super Brilliant FC.

Super Brilliant FC were practising for a

REALLY BiG GAME!

The next day they were playing against their greatest rivals: a team of sneering, jeering, rough, tough older kids called Nosebleed United...

Practice wasn't going too super-brilliantly.

Gurly-Gurl had broken a nail while playing in goal ...

... Posh Norris had crumpled his hat ...

... and Tuffnut was yelling at everyone because they always lost to Nosebleed United and it looked like it would happen *again*.

... out fell Gristle and Blemish.

CHAPTER TWO

Gristle and Blemish were Nosebleed United's dirtiest players, which means they were very dirty indeed. "Ha ha!" they laughed.

"You'll be crying like little babies who've lost their dollies when we beat you tomorrow," jeered Gristle.

"Stop spying on us and depart,"
demanded Posh Norris.

"Well, okay..." sneered Gristle.

"But we'll be back in a minute with the rest of the team!" snarled Blemish.

Off they scoffingly went, to fetch their scabby-kneed friends.

Frank called a team meeting.

After much huddling, Super Brilliant FC decided to practise somewhere else; somewhere a long way from Nosebleed United.

"I know," said Big Hair,

LET'S GO TO THE TSFF!

"PSPT!" said Uneasy. "What's that?"
"The Top Secret Footy Field, of
course!" said Big Hair.

Everyone agreed it was a Super Brilliant
Idea, and off they went...

PSST!
Check
This
OUT!

This WAY
To the
TOP
SeCReT
FOOTY
FieLD!

And Chapter
three, too!

CHAPTER THREE

Super Brilliant FC were halfway down Top Secret Footy Field Lane, when Uneasy took a left into Quitter Street.

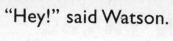

"Hey!" said Watson.

Where are you going?

"Home," said Uneasy, uneasily.

"But why, pray tell?" asked Bardy.

Uneasy explained that all the talk about toffees and lost dollies had made him so uneasy he didn't want to play any more.

"G-good luck tomorrow," he said, and away he ran before anyone could change his mind.

"Oh, great!" snarled Tuffnut.

Now we really don't stand a chance tomorrow!

"Tomorrow? What's happening tomorrow?" asked a small voice.

Big Hair jumped. "Who said that?" she gasped.

"Me!" said the voice. "Over here!" Everyone turned around.

It was Crumb, sitting on the steps of his little house.

Oh, hi Crumb!

Frank told Crumb about the game
against Nosebleed United.
And then he had an idea.

"Come off it, Frank!" scoffed Tuffnut.

"Size schmize! Of course he can," insisted Big Hair.

"Tuffnut's right." Crumb shrugged.

"You mean you've never, like, *tried* to play?" asked Gurly-Gurl.

Crumb nodded.

"Well, why not give it a bash?" said Posh Norris.

We are in great need of another player!

Crumb wondered what it would feel like to play for a change, instead of sitting and watching ...

... and decided it might feel pretty good.

"Okey-dokey," he said, jumping down the steps.

CHAPTER FOUR

Super Brilliant FC hurried on to the TSFF ...

... and Big Hair rolled the ball to Crumb.

"Give me a break!" scoffed Tuffnut.

There's no way he's gonna score!

Crumb took aim ...

... took a swing,

AND...

The ball wobbled, and that was that.

"Told you," sniffed Tuffnut. "He's rubbish!"
"Try again, Crumb," said Gurly-Gurl.

But totally whack it this time...

Crumb shook his head. "N-no thanks ...
I don't think so..."

"How about going in goal, then?"
suggested Watson.

Crumb thought about the same things he
thought about on page 21.

"All right then!" he said after a while.
"Maybe I'll be good at that!"

Crumb took his place in goal.

Gurly-Gurl and Frank took three shots each ...

... and scored every time — even when they were trying not to.

"Just like I said," sighed Tuffnut.

"Ignore him," said Frank. "Just try jumping around a bit more!"

But Crumb shook his head. "No, thanks," he said. "I'll just sit and watch."

CHAPTER FIVE

SUDDENLY...

AARGH! NO!

"Dudette! What's occurring?" asked Grungy Rockette. "LOOK!" shrieked Big Hair, pointing to the sky in horror.

It's raining!

More than anything in the world, Big Hair hated rain, because rain made her big hair go frizzy, and when her big hair got frizzy, it got twice as big!

"Quick! My house is the closest!" suggested Watson.

Let's go there until it stops!

Good idea!

Quick! Let's go!

But Tuffnut wasn't so sure. "Wait!" he said.

Tuffnut loved snacks, especially really big ones that most other people call meals.

"As a matter of fact, I do," said Watson. He told them about a triple-decker double-chocolate fudge cake he had baked that very morning. "It's cooling on my kitchen window sill," he said.

"Then what are we waiting for?" said Tuffnut.

But Crumb didn't move.

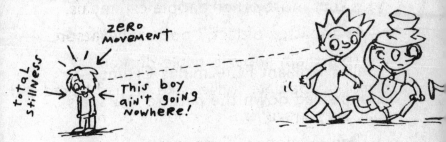

"Hey, Crumb..." said Frank.

"I-I'll catch up with you all later," said Crumb. "I've a few things to do, that's all."

Super Brilliant FC – minus Crumb – disappeared down the path to Watson's...

CHAPTER SIX

They hadn't gone far when Tuffnut had a suspicious thought. "Crumb's taking a short cut, I bet..."

...so he can get there first and scoff all the cake!

Having to share the cake was bad enough, but the idea of anyone eating it before him made Tuffnut's hands tighten into big fists.

I know! I'll beat Crumb to it and take a short cut myself!

When no one was looking, he snuck away across the Swampy Swamp...

WATSON'S HOUSE

SWAMPY SWAMP

DANGER

BEWARE of BOGGYNESS

SNEAK! SNEAK!

He was licking his lips and imagining
the chocolatey fudgy delights awaiting
him when, suddenly...

He stepped into a bog!

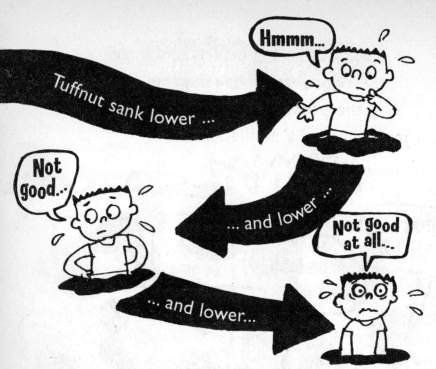

The bog was gloopy and boggy and in
seconds he was stuck up to his waist.

"Help me!" he yelled, as loud as he could.

MEANWHILE...

On the path to Watson's, Frank and his friends heard a muffled shout.

"Well, wherever he is, it sounds like he's in trouble!" observed Frank. "Come on!"

Off they ran as fast as they could, in the direction of Tuffnut's cries.

CHAPTER SEVEN

By the time Frank and his friends reached the swamp, Tuffnut was stuck up to his chest.

"What happened to you?" asked Frank.
"It's a long story," said Tuffnut. "But first..."

Posh Norris found a branch ...

... and Tuffnut grabbed it.

Frank grabbed
Posh Norris, and
Big Hair grabbed
Frank, and Grungy
Rockette grabbed Big
Hair, and Watson grabbed
Grungy Rockette, and Bardy
grabbed Watson, and Gurly-Gurl
grabbed Bardy.

they counted...

PULL!

They tugged ...

... and pulled ...

... and groaned ...

... and strained.

But Tuffnut didn't budge.

Oh no! My cake-scoffing days are over!

Frank wiped his brow.

"Frankly, it's not working," he said.

"Indubitably," agreed Posh Norris.

"In dooby what?" asked Grungy Rockette.

"Ignore him," said Watson. "He always uses words like that!"

The point is, we need more pulling power.

"I could run to town and get a hair drier – whoops! I mean ... some help," suggested Big Hair.

"You could," said Watson thoughtfully.

Suddenly Frank had an idea.

"Little Crumb?" spluttered Tuffnut. "Have you lost your marbles?"

"Tuffnut's got a point, old chap!" said Posh Norris.

"Maybe so..." agreed Watson, "but he may be our best hope!"

Frank rubbed his chin and imagined where *he*'d be right now, if he were Crumb.

"Aha!" he exclaimed at last. "I know!"

"Try to keep Tuffnut's spirits up," Frank yelled as he ran off, "and I'll be back with Crumb as soon as I can!"

CHAPTER EIGHT

Frank ran and ran until he reached Gloomy Hill. At the top of the hill stood the Sulking Tree.

Just as he suspected, there was Crumb, sitting on the droopiest branch.

"CRUMB!"

spluttered Frank.

We need you like a sausage needs mustard!

Me? Why? I'm useless...

Frank told Crumb about Tuffnut and the bog. "Too bad," sniffed Crumb. "What do you want me to do about it?"

It serves him right!

"Please, Crumb!" said Frank. "I know Tuffnut's a pain in the bottom, but aren't there some good things about him, too?"

NO!

Are you sure?

"Let's see..." said Crumb, and he tried his best to remember some good things about Tuffnut...

FiRST

he remembered
when Tuffnut
gave him a
toffee, which
would have been
nice if he hadn't
found it on the
sole of his shoe...

AND THEN

he remembered
when Tuffnut
lifted him on to
a roof to fetch
a ball, but forgot
to help him
down until two
days later...

AND THEN

Crumb remembered when they made chalk drawings on the pavement and Tuffnut said that Crumb's alien robot was the coolest drawing ever, and that he'd never be able to do anything like it in a million years.

All of a sudden, it stopped raining, and a warm little light went on in Crumb's heart.

Crumb jumped off the branch.

"Okey-doke!" he said. "I'll help."
"Thanks a zillion, Crumb!" said Frank.
"That's very big of you!"

This way, quick! To Chapter Nine!

CHAPTER NINE

When Frank and Crumb got back to the bog, Tuffnut was stuck up to his chin.

"Thank goodness!" said Tuffnut. "I don't know what's worse: sinking in a bog, or listening to Grungy's songs and Bardy's poems!"

We were just trying to keep your spirits up, dude!

Thy ingratitude doth sting like a thousand nettles upon my bare bottom!

And then Tuffnut turned to Crumb.
"Crumb," he pleaded. "Help me!"
"Only if you say 'please'!" said Crumb.

"Well, all right then..." said Crumb, and
he picked up the branch.

Tuffnut bit.

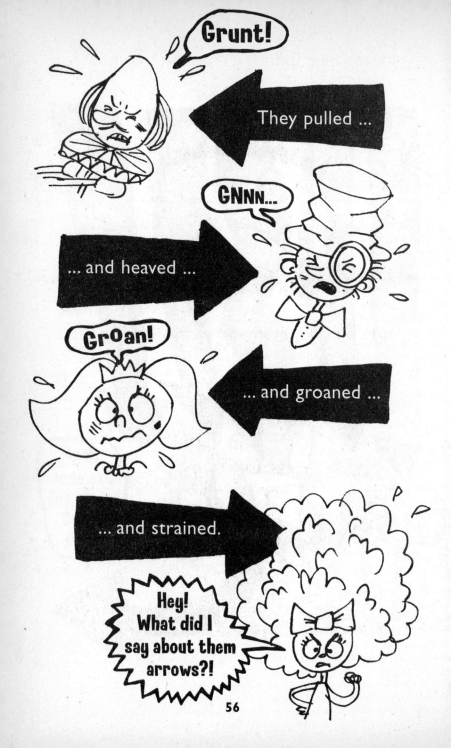

56

Meanwhile, Tuffnut gritted his teeth ...

... and bit and chomped with all his might...

"Thanks, Crumb!" panted Tuffnut. "You may be small, but you made a super-big difference!"

"Yes, I did, didn't I?" said Crumb.

And he grinned a big broad grin.

CHAPTER TEN

To celebrate his rescue, Tuffnut invited everyone to his house for a Thank-You-For-Rescuing-Me type party.

"And me?" said Crumb. "What can I bring?"

Tuffnut put an arm around him. "Just bring yourself," he said.

"Golly gosh! Thanks!" smiled Crumb.

And he fainted.

"Aah! How cute!" gushed Gurly-Gurl.

"The honour was too much for him!"

"Honour schmonour!" scoffed Big Hair.

"It was Tuffnut's boggy stench, more like!"

Tuffnut sniffed himself and quickly agreed.

"Come over in an hour," he said.

CHAPTER ELEVEN

When Crumb came to, he first of all felt dizzy, and then he felt FANTASTIC! He had never been a guest of honour before, and so he rushed home to change.

Rush!

Rush!

Crumb took a long time deciding exactly which red T-shirt to wear ...

By the time he reached Tuffnut's house, the party was in full swing. Crumb peeked through the letter box on tippy-toe.

Grungy Rockette
was playing "Purple
Haze" **very** loudly
on her guitar ...

... Big Hair was
playing a cruel
practical joke ...

... and Watson's cake
was sitting on a
special little table.

 "Ah! There it is!" sighed Crumb,

licking his lips.

And then Crumb noticed some words
written on top of the cake in icing.

"Golly gosh!" gasped Crumb.

Crumb saw something he didn't like one
teeny-weeny little bit.

CHAPTER TWELVE

Crumb had seen enough.

"There's no way I'm going to let Tuffnut spoil my big moment!" he seethed.

He pushed at the door, but it was locked!

Darn!

Crumb looked again. Tuffnut was bending down so low to sniff the cake, his nose was in the icing!

sniff! sniff!

Ahh! Sweet nectar!

Crumb searched desperately for the doorbell.

At last he found it ...

... but it was too high up for him to reach!

Crumb jumped ...

... and jumped ...

... and jumped again!

rRiNG!

And
then
Crumb
waited ...

... and waited ...

... and waited.

But still NO ONE answered!

Crumb glared through the letterbox and saw why.

No one could hear the bell because Grungy Rockette's guitar was louder than anything!

And then Crumb saw something that was

Tuffnut had seized the cake in his bare hands!

In desperation Crumb knocked at the door ...

RAT-A-TAT!

hAMMeR!
hAMMeR!

... and then he hammered at it ...

... and then he kicked it.

BAM!
BLAM!

But STILL no one answered!

NOTE TO READER:

Crumb kept on this ringing and bamming thing for quite a while. Re-read page 76 three times to get the idea, and then move on to the rest of this page.
Thank you!

AND Then...

just as Tuffnut was about to take a huge, gigantic, mega-bite...

KERRANG!

Grungy Rockette finished playing at last.

"Hey, listen!" said Watson.

What's that noise?

Ring!

Bam!

Ring!

Bam!

"Crikey!" gasped Frank.

Check this out!

79

Big Hair opened the door.

Crumb marched over to Tuffnut, grabbed
the cake, and kicked his shin.

Then Crumb shared the cake with everyone — including Tuffnut, who had arranged the whole Thank-You-For-Rescuing-Me-Type-Party, after all...

"Hey, Crumb?" said Frank as he munched his slice. "What are you up to tomorrow?"

Crumb wasn't sure.

"Sure schmure!" said Big Hair. "Come on, Crumb!"

Crumb thought for a moment. And then a warm little light went on in his eyes. "Golly gosh!" he beamed.

CHAPTER THIRTEEN

The next day, about halfway between lunch and supper, Super Brilliant FC met Nosebleed United.

"Ha ha!" sneered Blemish, pointing at Crumb.

"Prepare to be CRUSHED!" jeered Gristle.

Nosebleed United
huffed ...

... and puffed ...

... and hacked ...

... and whacked ...

... but Super Brilliant FC were

SuPeR BRiLLiANT!

Watson was awesomely speedy ...

... Gurly-Gurl was unbeatable ...

... Tuffnut was a tough nut ...

... and Big Hair was, well, Big Hair!

And Crumb? He was...

SPECTACULAR!

I'm befuddled!

RAZZLE! DAZZLE!

He dazzled as he dribbled...

He soared through the air...

AIR

SOAR

Oof!

And he kicked like a thunderbolt...

"Well played, you!" said Gristle wearily.
"You played well!" said Blemish blearily.

"Thank you," said Frank, "but to be frank..."

CHAPTER FOURTEEN

Now that the game was over, Nosebleed United and Super Brilliant FC headed down to The Greasy Slice for the tastiest pizza in Upsan Downs.

Super Brilliant FC had only enough money for one pizza pie to share ...

One pizza pie, please...

... while Nosebleed United bought themselves one each.

Nine pies and make it snappy!

"To prove there are no hard feelings," said Gristle to Frank, "if you lot are still hungry you can lick our pizza boxes clean!"

Nosebleed United thought that was very funny indeed.

"Erm ... excuse me?" asked Big Hair.

Nosebleed United stopped laughing and chuckling and sneering. "We don't know!" they shrugged.

Could it be because you all lost your favourite dollies when you were small?

Suddenly Nosebleed United looked very thoughtful and sad and serious. "Yes!" they said at last. "We did!"

"Just as I suspected," said Big Hair.

Mean people are often sad and angry about something bad that happened when they were itsy-bitsy people ...

... like losing their favourite dollies, for example!

Nosebleed United said that quite possibly Big Hair was right, now that they thought about it, and they started to cry and blub and say things like "Poor Dolly-wolly", and "Dolly gone bye-byes"...

MEANWHILE

Crumb crawled under the table and tied an awful lot of knots...

By the time he'd finished, the pizzas were ready.

Nosebleed United suddenly stopped blubbing.
"Oi!" yelled Blemish. "Those pizzas are ours!"

"Well, catch us if you can," chuckled Big Hair. "
They jumped to their feet ...

... and tumbled down in a heap!